QUICKREADS

SOUNDS OF TERROR

ANNE SCHRAFF

SADDLEBACK
EDUCATIONAL PUBLISHING

QUICKREADS

SERIES 1

Black Widow Beauty
Danger on Ice
Empty Eyes
The Experiment
The Kula'i Street Knights
The Mystery Quilt
No Way to Run
The Ritual
The 75-Cent Son
The Very Bad Dream

SERIES 2

The Accuser
Ben Cody's Treasure
Blackout
The Eye of the Hurricane
The House on the Hill
Look to the Light
Ring of Fear
The Tiger Lily Code
Tug-of-War
The White Room

SERIES 3

The Bad Luck Play
Breaking Point
Death Grip
Fat Boy
No Exit
No Place Like Home
The Plot
Something Dreadful Down Below
Sounds of Terror
The Woman Who Loved a Ghost

SERIES 4

The Barge Ghost
Beasts
Blood and Basketball
Bus 99
The Dark Lady
Dimes to Dollars
Read My Lips
Ruby's Terrible Secret
Student Bodies
Tough Girl

SADDLEBACK
EDUCATIONAL PUBLISHING
www.sdlback.com

ISBN-13: 978-1-61651-206-4
ISBN-10: 1-61651-206-7
eBook: 978-1-60291-928-0

Printed in Guangzhou, China
0411/04-80-11

15 14 13 12 11   2 3 4 5 6

■ ■ ■

When he first saw it, Philip Sanchez couldn't believe it. He was standing in front of his grandparents' mobile home in southern Florida. About 100 feet ahead, the earth itself seemed in motion! "What is that?" he gasped. "What's happening?"

Abuelo Ramon, Philip's grandfather, laughed and said, "The crabs are coming in from the mangrove. They come in just so far, and then they return. It is a nightly ritual for them."

Now Philip could make out the small spider-like crabs, waving their little claws in the air. "That's *weird!*" he said with a shudder. He didn't like living here in southern Florida.

He didn't like the bugs or the humidity. And he certainly saw nothing to like about these crabs!

But Philip's only parent, his mother, had been sentenced to 18 months in jail for drug dealing in Los Angeles. There'd been nowhere for Philip to go except here with his grandparents.

"Don't worry, *nieto,*" Grandfather said, "the crabs are harmless."

It grieved Grandfather greatly when Philip's mother went to prison. But now he concentrated on helping Philip. "This is a good place, Philip. No gangs or drugs—like where you were. The people here are good," he said.

"It wasn't all bad in the *barrio,*" Philip said. "I had lots of good friends. I never got into the bad stuff." Sadly, Philip's mother got mixed up with drugs through her boyfriend, Ricky. She didn't know what she was getting into. Not until it was too late, and the police snapped handcuffs on her.

The sun was going down. *Abuela* Carmen

smiled at Philip and said, "Look, honey. The sky is so pretty here."

"Yeah," Philip said. He appreciated his grandparents' kindness. But he missed Los Angeles and the *barrio*. Only one good thing had happened here so far. That was meeting Cindy Bigelow, a pretty junior at Pine River High School.

As darkness fell, shrill sounds came from the mangrove.

"It's only the wildcats," *Abuelo* said.

But Philip heard something else. He heard the distinct sound of a woman crying bitterly. He looked at his grandparents. *Abuela* looked distressed. "Oh, that's nothing," she said. "It's just a strange wind that blows through an empty home at the end of the street. Nobody pays any attention to it." But as his grandmother spoke, Philip saw her lower lip trembling.

■ ■ ■

"It sure doesn't *sound* like wind," Philip said. "It sounds like some poor lady who's really hurting."

"It's the wind," *Abuela* said firmly. "Come on in now. I'm making tamales, the kind you like, *nieto!*"

Grandfather looked thoughtful as they ate dinner. "We never knew the people in the green house—the one that's empty now. That's where the wind makes the strange noise. But the other people in the park are very nice."

After dinner, Philip went out for a walk around the trailer court.

"Watch out for the no-see-ums," his grandmother warned. "You know—they are those tiny swarming insects that get in your nose, your eyes—even your mouth, if it's open!"

As Philip walked, moonlight flooded the park. He glanced at the neat rows of mobile homes and their tidy little yards. Colorful flowers grew everywhere. He couldn't hear the wildcats anymore. Maybe they'd finished their argument and finally gone to bed.

But, as Philip drew closer to the green

home, he heard the woman's loud sobbing again. Her voice floated from the open windows. Philip stared at the run-down home. It was surrounded by dead hibiscus shrubs. The voice inside rose and fell like the waves of the ocean. First her sobs would rise to a crescendo like the high tide. Then the loud sobs would die down, and there would be soft weeping—like water lapping the sand. To Philip's ears, both sounds were cries of pure terror.

Philip's mother cried like that when Ricky would beat her. Philip would clench his fists and want to die! But he knew that if he tried to interfere, Ricky would just hurt Mom more.

The abuse never did stop, because Mom wouldn't call the police. Even when Ricky hurt her so bad she had to go to the hospital. Then she'd make up lies about falling down the steps. It didn't end until both Ricky and Mom were arrested. Ricky was dealing big time. He got eight years in prison.

It broke Philip's heart to see his mother going off to prison. But at least Ricky wasn't hurting her anymore. There would be no more black eyes and swollen jaws, no more concussions. She wouldn't have to spend so many nights rolled up in a pathetic, sobbing little ball in her bed, crying from pain and humiliation.

Now Philip stood in the darkness, staring at the green mobile home. He couldn't help wondering: Was another bad man getting away with hurting a woman in there?

■ ■ ■

Philip remembered what his grandfather had told him. *"The people here are good."*

But that wasn't true of anywhere. There were both good and bad people in all places. Back in the *barrio,* even amidst the gangbangers and dealers, there were plenty of good, hardworking people.And, though he was just 17 years old, Philip knew there had to be people like that here in Pine River.

As Philip stood there, a silver-haired lady came out of her mobile home across the street.

"Hi," Philip said. "Do you know if anybody lives in this green house?"

The woman shook her head. "No, it's abandoned. What a mess! They ought to just burn it down!" she said.

■ ■ ■

When Philip got to school the next morning, he looked for one of the two friends he'd made since coming here. One was a Vietnamese boy named Moon. The other was Cindy. He saw Moon first.

"You liking Pine River any better?" Moon asked as the boys walked down the hall to their first class. Moon's family had come to the United States when he was just a baby. Now he was a regular American kid. He was a good shortstop for the Pine River Patriots.

"I don't know. Last night there were a million crabs at the park, and wildcats were screaming—" Philip said.

Moon laughed. "I think all the wild life around here is cool."

Philip wanted to tell Moon about the crying woman, but he didn't want to seem foolish so he didn't say anything.

At lunch, Cindy asked Philip where he lived. He felt self-conscious about mentioning the park. He knew that her family lived in Little River, a fancy development. "Oh, near the river," he said. He didn't want Cindy to think he was "trailer trash."

"You told me you live with your grandparents," Cindy said. "Are your parents divorced?"

Philip felt uneasy. "Dad's dead, and Mom's, uh—sick, but she'll get better," he said.

"My mom's dead, too. She drowned when I was eight," Cindy said. "Dad married my stepmom when I was eleven. She's okay. She's a real estate agent. She got Dad into that business, too. They make lots more money than Dad did selling water softener systems."

"That's great," Philip said.

"So you live near the river, huh?" Cindy pressed. "Say—you don't live in that big mobile home park, do you?"

Philip's heart sank. Cindy's house was in a gated community! Now Philip was supposed to confess that he lived in that tacky mobile home park. Cindy would know that most of the people there were poor. Nearly all of the older people were living on pensions. And lots of the younger families were on welfare. Philip felt like he *was* trailer trash. He was sure that once Cindy found out, she wouldn't want to be his friend anymore.

■ ■ ■

Philip couldn't lie, though. "Yeah, I live in the mobile home park. But, when Mom gets better, we'll be moving to a real house."

"I used to live in that park, too," Cindy said, shocking Philip. "My mom and dad lived there when they didn't have much money. It's not a bad place. I made lots of friends there. But it was sad after Mom died—so we moved."

Relieved, Philip grinned back at her. "Yeah, there's lots of wildlife around there, too," he said.

"I remember all the birds flying to the mangrove," Cindy said. "Are your grandparents nice, Philip?"

"Oh, yeah, they're great," Philip said. Cindy smiled and reached over to pat Philip's shoulder. "You're so nice and real," she said. "So many boys are show-offs, Philip. I'm really glad we're friends."

Philip was getting happy goose bumps when he suddenly spotted a sullen-looking boy standing nearby. The guy was staring at them. "Who's that giving us the evil eye?" he asked.

"Oh, that's Steve. Don't pay any attention to him. He's creepy. I wouldn't date him if he was the only boy in school," Cindy said with feeling. "But he won't take no for an answer."

Philip smiled. All of a sudden Pine River was looking pretty cool.

■ ■ ■

After school, Philip waited for the bus. He was surprised when a late-model pickup pulled near him. Steve leaned out and said, "Want a ride?"

"Uh, yeah, thanks," Philip said, climbing up into the cab.

"Hey, you live out in the trailer park, right?" Steve asked.

"Yeah, the mobile home park," Philip said. He felt funny. Already he was sorry for accepting this ride.

Then Steve's expression turned hard.

"I checked you out, Sanchez," he said in a nasty voice. "You can't fool me. I know all about you."

Philip could feel Steve's hatred surrounding him like a poisonous laser beam, frying his brains.

"Yeah, man, my father is a whiz on computers. All I had to do was get some social security numbers off your records at school. Then we traced you to your old school in L.A. After that we accessed the newspapers to find out why you left town so quick. And sure enough, we found out about the drug bust, your mom going to prison—the whole thing," Steve said.

"You had no right to look at my personal files!" Philip stammered. He had always thought that school records were supposed to be confidential!

"So sue me," Steve laughed. "I found out you're *scum,* Sanchez! You got a lot of nerve thinking you can hook up with a classy girl like Cindy."

Philip felt a terrible pounding in his head. He thought he was going to be sick.

■ ■ ■

"**H**ere's the deal, Sanchez," Steve said. "I was making headway with Cindy before you showed up. You messed it up for me. So you just break it off with her, and my lips are sealed. Nobody has to know about your dirty past. There must be some low-class chicks out at the trailer park you can snare. You know— high school dropouts, losers. Some girls who are more your style."

Philip was furious. "Cindy said she wouldn't date you if you were the last guy in school!" he snapped.

Steve gripped the wheel tightly. The blood vessels in his temples were bulging out. "You kiss her off, man! If you don't, I'll make sure every kid at school knows who you are!" he said.

Halfway to the mobile home park, Steve ground to a stop, gouging out gravel from the shoulder of the road. "Get out, Sanchez! You can walk the rest of the way. Tomorrow at school, you break it off with Cindy. Or I'll make sure you won't have a single friend at Pine River High. You'll be a *pariah!*" Steve said.

Philip jumped from the cab and Steve took off, spraying Philip with gravel as he drove away.

Philip trudged toward home, his heart aching. Cindy *might* still be his friend when she learned of Mom's drug bust. But he knew her parents wouldn't like it a bit.

Philip desperately needed to talk to somebody, but who? He didn't have Moon's phone number.

If he told his grandparents, he knew what they would say.

"Philip, you are a good boy. You are as good as any boy on this earth, and you don't need to be ashamed of anything. Your mother made a terrible mistake—but that's not your fault. Hold your head high and be proud. Whoever does not want to be your friend because of your mother's crime is not worth having as a friend. You have always been a fine boy, Philip. You will do great things in this world, and don't you ever forget it. Anybody is lucky to be your friend!"

He knew he could count on them. But he could just imagine the corridors of Pine River High buzzing with gossip about his mom. It would be awful! Philip would be ashamed to show his face.

Loneliness and sadness closed in around Philip like a shroud. When he passed the green mobile home on the corner, he was lost in his own misery. But then he heard her. The woman's mournful sobs stopped him cold. Somehow he felt his own sorrow mingling in a terrible way with the wails of the unseen woman.

■ ■ ■

"Grandma," Philip said that night, "I hear that woman crying again." *Abuela* looked up sharply. "It is only the wildcats." Her voice was trembling.

"No, I'm sure I hear a woman's voice," Philip insisted. "You have to walk down there with me, Grandma. You'll hear it clearly then. Maybe somebody is in trouble and needs our help!"

"There is no one in trouble, *bobo,*" Grandma scolded. But she slipped on a sweater to go out. Grandma was 72 years old, but she was still fit and strong. There were only a few gray threads in her jet black hair. Philip thought she was a very handsome woman. He saw his mother's remarkable beauty in his grandmother's fine, high cheekbones and luminous eyes.

When the pair walked down the street to the green house, there was only silence. "You see?" Grandmother said. "You are imagining things, Philip. Let's go now." She sounded rather relieved.

"Wait a little bit," Philip pleaded. "Maybe she'll start crying again—like she was before."

"Come, let's go home. There is no one in that place," Grandma said.

But then, as they stood there, it began again. The sobs started softly, then rose in a shattering crescendo.

"Oh, *santo Dios!*" Grandmother cried, grasping Philip's hand. "We must go home at once. It is *aparecidos*—ghosts!"

"But what if somebody in there needs help?" Philip asked.

"No, Philip! There is no one in there," Grandmother said, dragging him away with amazing strength. "But you must not come here again—ever!"

That night, after Philip went to bed, he heard his grandparents talking in their room.

"It is the *aparecidos,* Ramon!" Grandmother said.

"Maybe it is only the wind—like everyone says," Grandfather said.

"I don't think so. Something awful must

have happened in that house," Grandmother said.

Philip lay in bed, thinking about what he had to do tomorrow. He would tell Cindy everything before Steve had the chance to broadcast his ugly story. If Cindy was half as wonderful as he thought, she would understand.

In the morning, right after he got off the bus, Philip saw Cindy with two friends. "Cindy, come over this way. We need to talk!" he called out.

"Philip, you look so serious," Cindy said, following him to the quad.

"Steve is mad because we're friends, Cindy. He dug into my life and found out that my mom was arrested for drugs in Los Angeles. He threatened to use that information against me. *I* did nothing wrong! But my mom made a big mistake, and now she's in prison." Philip watched the girl closely to judge her reaction.

Cindy's eyes opened wide and her mouth dropped open.

■ ■ ■

"What happened with your mom isn't your fault," Cindy said when Philip finished his story.

"Cindy, I've never used drugs in my life," Philip insisted.

"That's—wonderful," Cindy said. She was blinking rapidly. Of course she was shocked. Philip had expected that. He desperately searched her face for some reassuring sign that they were still friends—that nothing had changed. But then he realized he was asking too much. He had to give her time.

"I'll see you at lunch, okay?" Philip asked softly.

"Yes. At lunch," Cindy said. She hurried away then, joining the girls she had been talking to earlier. All of them seemed to go right into an animated conversation. But Cindy's two friends were now glancing over at Philip.

Surely Cindy wasn't telling them what he'd just told her!

As Philip walked to his first class, he spotted Steve. "Don't bother ratting me out to Cindy. I already told her everything," Philip said bitterly.

Steve's mouth dropped open and Philip turned and walked away.

At lunchtime, Philip waited for Cindy, but she didn't come. After a few minutes, a friend of hers rushed over to him. She said that Cindy and a couple other girls had to go to a meeting.

It was a lie, of course.

Philip was eating his macaroni lunch by himself when Moon joined him.

"Not hungry? Doesn't look like you're eating much," Moon said.

Philip blurted out the whole story.

"I already heard it this morning," Moon interrupted.

"You mean it's all over school already?" Philip gasped.

"Yeah, man, but don't sweat it," Moon said. "It's big news today. But in another couple days some other gossip will take its place. Trust me. This is your 90 seconds of bad fame."

"Cindy and I are through, though," Philip said. "We're history. I know it."

"Don't be too hard on the chick. She's got a real straight-arrow father. He's like a drill sergeant. One time he thought she was doing marijuana and he went ballistic. He's a tough dude, Philip. No way could she hang with a guy whose mom got busted for drugs," Moon said.

"But it's not fair," Philip groaned. "It's not like *I* did something wrong!"

"Look, Philip," Moon said. "One day last spring Cindy came to school with cuts on her nose, and she was missing her glasses. The rap was that her father smacked her across the face for backtalking him. She got the cuts on her nose when he busted her glasses. If you were a sixteen-year-old girl, would you cross a mean dude like that?"

Philip was stunned. He felt sick to his stomach.

■ ■ ■

Moon drove Philip home that day. As they passed the green mobile home, Philip said, "That's the place where I keep hearing this weird sound—like a woman crying."

"Yeah, I know. It's the ghost lady," Moon said.

"You *know* about her?" Philip asked.

"Sure. I heard about it right after we moved to Pine River. Couple of us tried to sneak in and see what was going on. But the place is deserted," Moon said.

■ ■ ■

At school the next day, Philip caught up to Cindy before English class. He wanted to hear from her own lips that she didn't want anything more to do with him. As much as that would hurt him, *not* knowing was hurting him even more.

"We're not friends anymore—right, Cindy?" he asked.

Cindy looked down at the tops of her

shoes. "Yeah, sure we are," she mumbled.

"Cindy, please don't jerk me around," Philip said. "Just tell me the truth. I don't want you ducking me and acting weird. Just tell me we're not friends anymore, and I swear I won't bother you ever again." Philip could feel his heart breaking.

Pain showed on Cindy's face. Her eyes were filled with tears. "Philip, I'm really sorry. I liked you more than any boy I've ever known. I still do. But my parents, I mean my dad—he doesn't want me seeing you," she said.

"I understand," Philip said. "It's okay." He wasn't mad at her. In fact he pitied her. "I won't bother you anymore."

"I'm so sorry!" Cindy cried.

Moon promised to drive Philip home every day. He offered to get Philip a job at the fitness center where he worked. Then Philip could save up for a car of his own.

As Philip and Moon walked to Moon's car after school, a gleaming Lexus pulled into the lot. The beautiful woman at the wheel wore dark glasses, even though it was a cloudy day. "Cindy's stepmom picks her up," Moon said.

"I hate this whole place," Philip said bitterly. "I hate the crabs and the mosquitoes and the wildcats. I hate the snobby rich people who live in Little River and look down their noses at people like me."

Moon added, "We've got to deal with it. It's the same all over. But don't envy the little girl who just got into that Lexus, man. She might live in a fancy house in Little River and get picked up by a lady driving a Lexus. But believe me, Philip, she's got bigger problems than you have."

■ ■ ■

"Like what?" Philip asked.

"Like her father," Moon said. "He's a real mean dude, and that's not a happy home she lives in."

As they passed the green mobile home, there were no sounds coming from inside. But an idea occurred to Philip. "Why don't we just go in and take a quick look around?"

he said. He needed some way to distract himself from brooding over Cindy. "Maybe some poor homeless lady has taken shelter in there, and she's crying from hunger. Or maybe she's sick."

"Come on, Philip!" Moon scoffed. "There's nobody in there."

"Just stop for a few minutes. We can run around the back and look for a way to get in," Philip pleaded.

"Okay," Moon sighed. "I must be nuts—but okay."

The weeds in back were knee-high. The door was stuck shut, but they didn't have to work long to push it open. Most of the furniture was gone. Only a few kitchen appliances remained.

Philip was tense, waiting for the woman to start crying. He wasn't sure what he'd do if that happened. Peeping in some of the cupboard doors, he found a few old boxes and a stack of junk mail. There were flyers advertising a water softener company. He stuck one of the flyers in his back pocket.

His heart was pounding with excitement, but he didn't say anything about it to Moon.

Then the sobbing began. The sounds were heartbreaking cries of pain. Moon and Philip looked at each other. They half-expected a tormented female ghost to rise like smoke from the peeling walls!

But they didn't see anything. Suddenly, both boys raced for the door at once. They almost knocked each other down trying to both get out.

The evil in that house was *real*. You could feel it, smell it. It was as if the house sheltered some horrible old secret, maybe a monstrous crime. It was as if evil itself lived in the gathering dust on the floors, in the hanging cobwebs on the ceiling, everywhere.

Now, slowly, Philip pulled the water softener flyer from his pocket. He held it up for Moon to read.

"You mean—nah—*they* lived in this house?" Moon said.

"Yeah," Philip said. "The Bigelows. Cindy told me her parents lived in the mobile home park when she was little. It must have been the green house. Otherwise, all these water softener flyers wouldn't have the name 'Thomas Bigelow' printed on them!"

■ ■ ■

On Saturday morning, the boys went to the library to do some computer research. The first thing they searched was the obituaries.

They found the article about Nancy Bigelow. She had died while on vacation with her husband in Key West. She'd suddenly disappeared while swimming in the ocean. Her body had never been recovered. A week later, the distraught widower had returned to Pine River alone. The family's young daughter had been away at summer camp when the tragedy occurred.

A later newspaper story reported Thomas Bigelow's marriage to local real estate agent Betty Trevor. The next month there was a story about the Bigelows winning a real estate sales award. The last story they found was about irate neighbors at the mobile home park calling a meeting. They were trying to get Bigelow to either fix up the mobile home he owned, or take it away.

As the boys drove home, Philip said, "I wouldn't be surprised if he hit his first wife—like he hit Cindy."

"Yeah. The second Mrs. Bigelow was probably hiding a black eye behind those dark glasses," Moon said grimly. "He sure could be a chronic abuser."

"Moon, remember when we were in that green mobile home? I noticed there was a funny concrete extension on the patio by the back door," Philip said. "It was sorta sloppy—"

Moon's eyes narrowed. "You think she's still there, don't you? Crying out for somebody to give her justice," he said.

■ ■ ■

The boys went to the police station with their story. The lieutenant seemed skeptical, but he promised to check it out.

One week later, Nancy Bigelow's remains were found. Just as Philip had suspected, she was buried behind the green mobile home in the patio cement. When Thomas Bigelow was arrested, he broke down immediately. It was a terrible accident, he said. His wife had fallen and struck her head on a marble table-top. He was so frightened of being blamed, he buried her in the yard and covered her body with cement. Then, pretending that Nancy was with him, he rushed to Key West. That was when and where he'd concocted the drowning story.

Nancy Bigelow was finally laid to rest on a grassy hill overlooking a lake. After the graveside service, Philip and his grandparents embraced Cindy and her stepmother. They needed good friends now, and the Sanchez family was there to offer that friendship.

The sounds of terror in the green mobile home were gone forever. The crying woman was now at peace, her spirit gone to her Maker.

After-Reading Wrap-Up

1. Who is the most interesting person in this story? Why?

2. One of Philip's problems was being unable to see Cindy. Nancy Bigelow's problem was not finding justice. Explain how finding Nancy Bigelow's body solved *both* problems.

3. How did the author make southern Florida *different* from Philip's home in Los Angeles? Name three details from the story. What was the *same* in both places?

4. What information about Philip did Steve and his dad use to uncover Philip's past?

5. What did Nancy Bigelow and Philip's mom have in common?

6. What might have happened if Philip had given in to Steve and broken off with Cindy? Would that decision have been true to Philip's character?